THE HOUSE I'LL BUILD FOR THE WRENS

by **Shirley Neitzel**

pictures by
Nancy Winslow Parker

SCHOLASTIC INC.
New York Toronto London Auckland Sydney

There are ten species of wren that breed in North America. The three species that build their nests in birdhouses made by people are the house wren (<u>Troglodytes aëdon</u>), Bewick's wren (<u>Thryomanes bewickii</u>), and the Carolina wren (<u>Thryothorus ludovicianus</u>).
A wren house should be made of pine or spruce. It should not be painted a bright color. Wrens do not like a house that swings.

For my father,
Theophilus Koehler
—S. N.

For Diane,
Central Park bird-watcher
—N. W. P

ISBN 0-590-22745-9

12 11 10 9 8 7 6 5 4 3 2 1   8 9/9 0 1 2 3/0

Printed in the U.S.A.   24

First Scholastic printing, September 1998

Watercolor paints, colored pencils, and a black pen were used for the full-color art. The text type is Seagull Light.

Here is the house I'll build for the wrens.

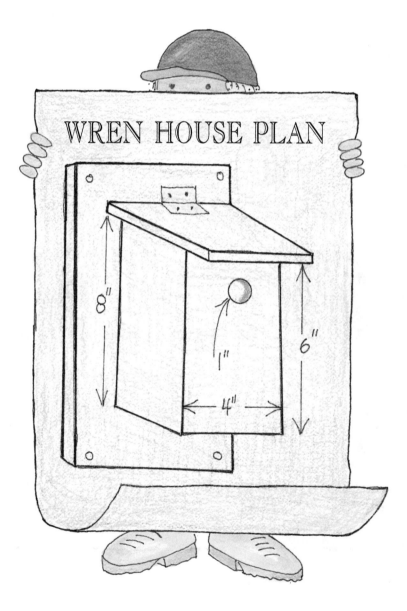

Here is the toolbox with all of the stuff

for the  I'll build for the wrens.

Here are the boards, just big enough,

I found near the 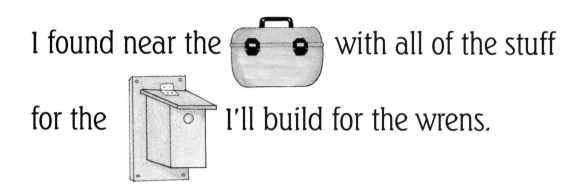 with all of the stuff

for the I'll build for the wrens.

Here is the rule, with joints that bend,

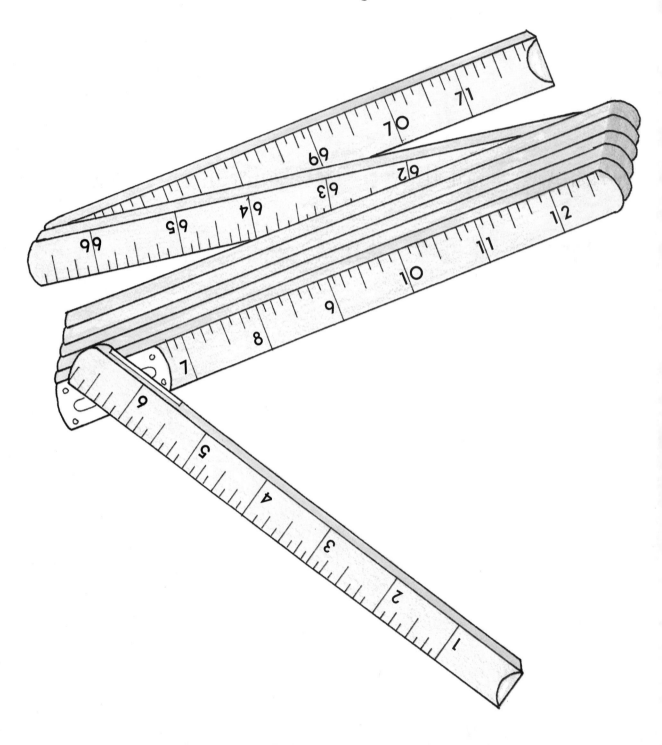

that measured the 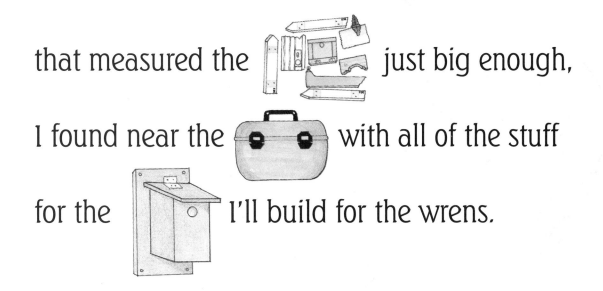 just big enough,

I found near the with all of the stuff

for the I'll build for the wrens.

Here is the hammer,

with a claw on the end,

beside the 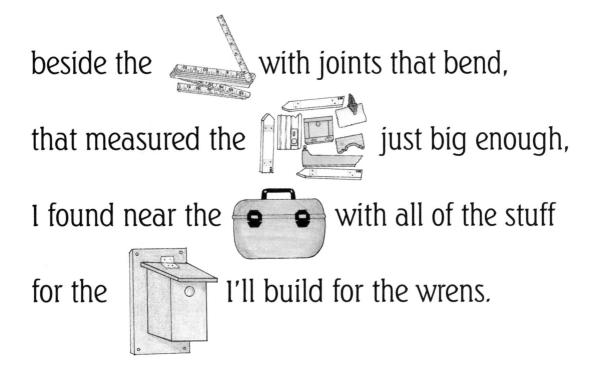 with joints that bend,

that measured the just big enough,

I found near the with all of the stuff

for the I'll build for the wrens.

Here is the sandpaper,
for smoothing the knot,

under the 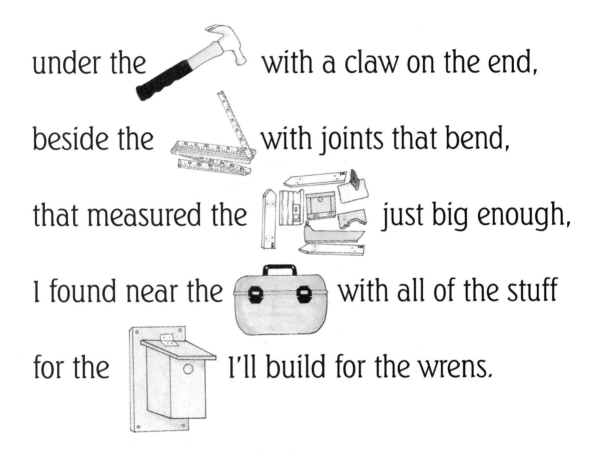 with a claw on the end,

beside the with joints that bend,

that measured the just big enough,

I found near the with all of the stuff

for the I'll build for the wrens.

Here are the nails (I'll need quite a lot)

next to the 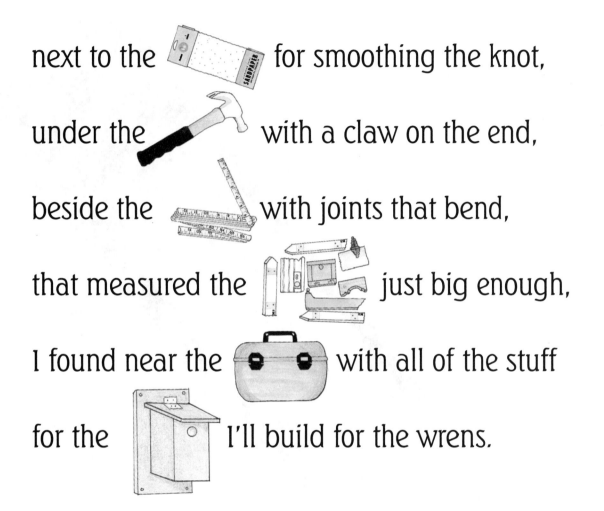 for smoothing the knot,

under the with a claw on the end,

beside the with joints that bend,

that measured the just big enough,

I found near the with all of the stuff

for the I'll build for the wrens.

Here is the level, with a bubble inside,

along with the 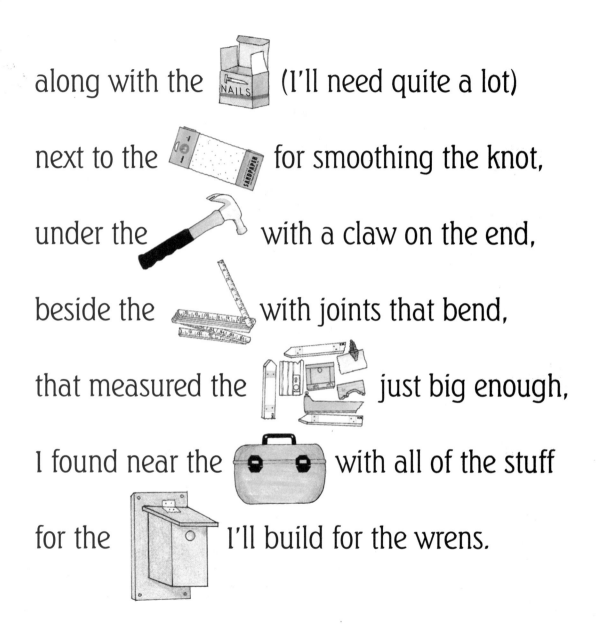 NAILS (I'll need quite a lot)

next to the SANDPAPER for smoothing the knot,

under the hammer with a claw on the end,

beside the ruler with joints that bend,

that measured the wood just big enough,

I found near the toolbox with all of the stuff

for the birdhouse I'll build for the wrens.

Here is the brush, two inches wide,

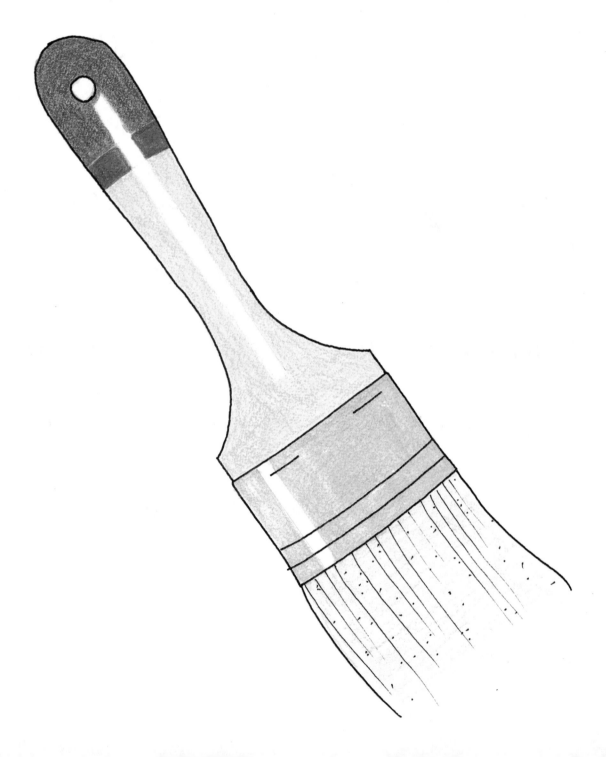

I found by the 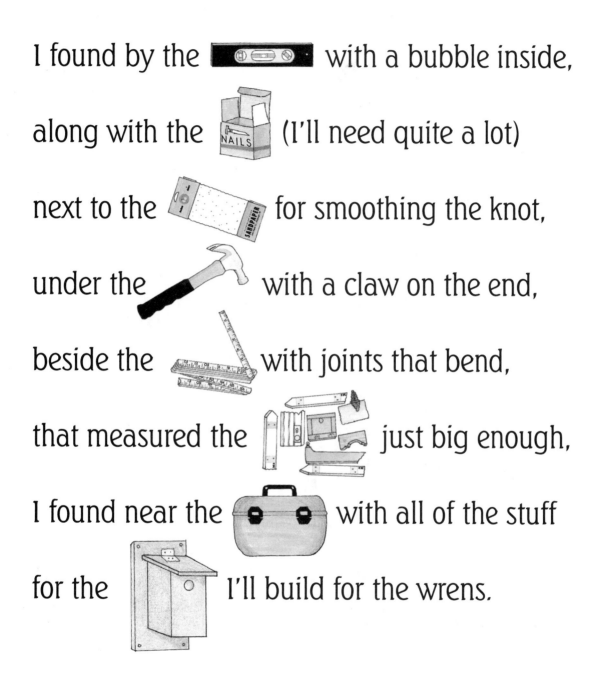 with a bubble inside,

along with the NAILS (I'll need quite a lot)

next to the SANDPAPER for smoothing the knot,

under the with a claw on the end,

beside the with joints that bend,

that measured the just big enough,

I found near the with all of the stuff

for the I'll build for the wrens.

Here is the paint, a nice blue shade,

I'll spread with the 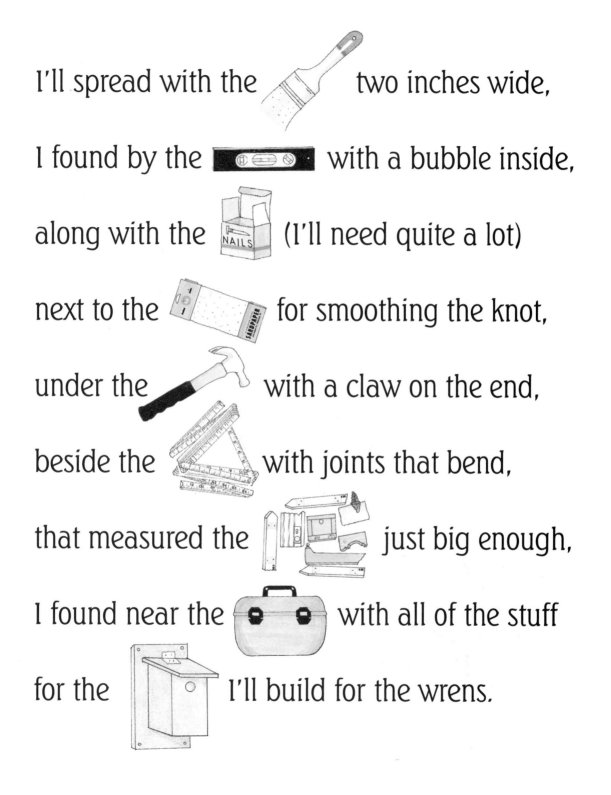 two inches wide,

I found by the with a bubble inside,

along with the NAILS (I'll need quite a lot)

next to the SANDPAPER for smoothing the knot,

under the with a claw on the end,

beside the with joints that bend,

that measured the just big enough,

I found near the with all of the stuff

for the I'll build for the wrens.

Here is the screwdriver with a flat blade

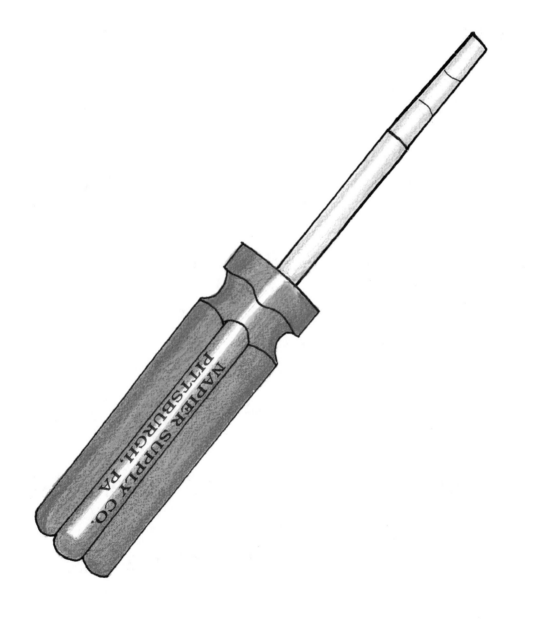

to open the 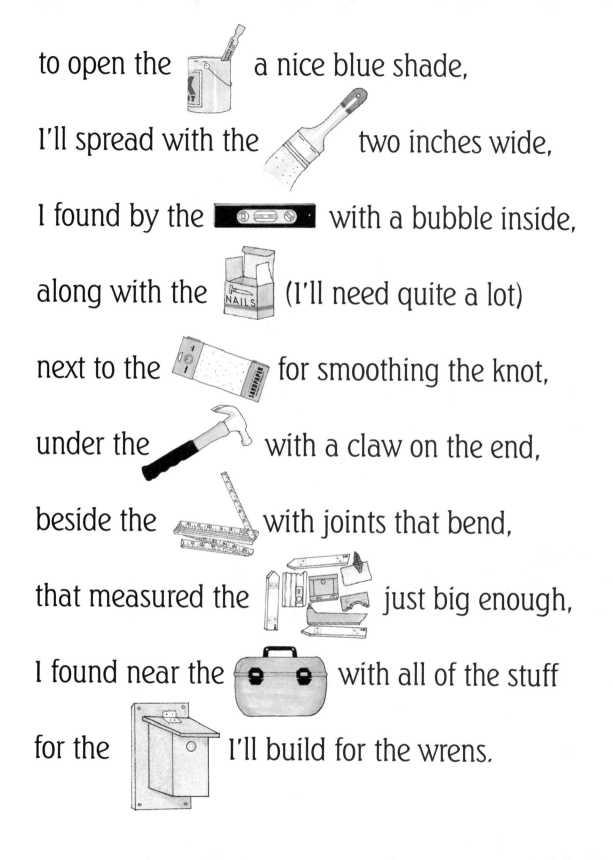 a nice blue shade,

I'll spread with the two inches wide,

I found by the with a bubble inside,

along with the NAILS (I'll need quite a lot)

next to the SANDPAPER for smoothing the knot,

under the with a claw on the end,

beside the with joints that bend,

that measured the just big enough,

I found near the with all of the stuff

for the I'll build for the wrens.

Here is my mother,
who stood at the door.

She looked at her toolbox
and also the floor.

I put back the hammer,
sandpaper, and rule,

wiped paint from the level,
screwdriver, and stool.

Then I washed the brush
and picked up each nail

and put the lid back
on the blue paint pail.

"A job well done!"
Mother said with pride.

"Let's take your creation
and hang it outside!

"You've built a fine house for the wrens."